The
PRAYER
of JABEZ
for Kids

The
PRAYER
of JABEZ
for Kids

By Dr. Bruce Wilkinson
Adapted by Melody Carlson
Illustrated by Dan Brawner

Tommy
NELSON®
Thomas Nelson, Inc.
Nashville

THE PRAYER OF JABEZ FOR KIDS

published in Nashville, Tennessee, by Tommy Nelson®,
a Division of Thomas Nelson, Inc.

Scripture quoted from the Holy Bible, New King James Version (NKJV),
© 1984 by Thomas Nelson, Inc.

Library of Congress Cataloging-in-Publication Data
Wilkinson, Bruce.
     The prayer of Jabez / originated by Bruce H. Wilkinson ; adapted
by Melody Carlson ; illustrated by Dan Brawner.
        p. cm.
     Summary: Recounts the Biblical story of Jabez and describes how his
prayer to God can be used by today's children to enrich their lives.
     ISBN 0-8499-7944-7
     1. Bible. O.T. Chronicles, 1st, IV, 10—Prayers—History and criticism—
Juvenile literature. 2. Christian children—Religious life—Juvenile literature.
3. Jabez (Biblical figure)—Juvenile literature. 4. Prayer—Christianity—Juvenile
literature. [1. Bible stories—O.T. 2. Jabez (Biblical figure) 3. Prayer. 4. Christian
life.] I. Wilkinson, Bruce. Prayer of Jabez. II. Brawner, Dan, ill. III. Title.
BS1345.6.P68 C37 2001
222'.6309505—dc21

                                   2001031269

Design: Koechel Peterson & Associates

Printed in the United States of America
01 02 03 04 05 WRZ 9 8 7 6 5 4

Contents

The Prayer of Jabez for Kids is dedicated to my four grandsons—Andrew, Eric, Johnny, and Jonathan David—who I pray will grow up to not only pray the prayer of Jabez but also become an example of the Jabez life. It has been a thrill to watch them grow under the wise leadership and love of their parents, and I look forward to being a part of their lives as they become men of Jabez for the next generation!

—Bruce Wilkinson

CHAPTER ONE
Little Prayer, Giant Prize

Who wants a life that's just plain ordinary? Wouldn't you rather have one that's filled with adventure, excitement, and lots of fun? Well, as it turns out, that's just the kind of life God wants for you, too. And it's the kind of life He promises each of us. It doesn't matter how young or old we are, God has something incredibly special for everyone—starting right now!

As a young man, I loved God, but I wondered how I could serve Him better. I wasn't sure what I wanted to do in the future. Maybe you know how that feels. On some

Jabez asks God for help.

days you might think you'd like to be an NFL quarterback or perhaps a famous ballet dancer. On other days you might even imagine yourself as a missionary tramping through a steaming jungle.

When we're young, we dream all kinds of possibilities. But when it's time to really choose, which way do we go? That's how I felt: What should I do with my life? How could I be more and do more for God?

At that time, a friend said, "Do you want something bigger and greater for your life?" Of

course I did. That's when my friend introduced me to a guy from the Bible named Jabez (pronounced JAY-behz).

Do you want something bigger and greater for your life?

He started with one short line from the Bible (1 Chronicles 4:9). Here's how it goes: "Now, Jabez was more honorable than his brothers." So then my friend explained how this ordinary guy, Jabez,

prayed that he might *be more and do more for God* (and remember, that's what I wanted too). My friend finished by saying that God granted Jabez his request. And that was the end of the story. Pretty short story, huh? And yet, somehow I knew it was a really big deal!

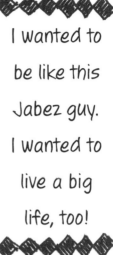

I wanted to be like this Jabez guy. I wanted to live a big life, too!

Right then and there, I decided I wanted to be like this Jabez guy. I wanted to live a big life, too! So I decided to find out more about Jabez for myself. I opened up my Bible and read all there was to read about Jabez:

> Now Jabez was more honorable than his brothers, and his mother called his name Jabez, saying, "Because I bore him in pain." And Jabez called on the God of Israel saying, "Oh, that You would bless me indeed, and enlarge my territory, that Your hand

would be with me, and that You would keep me from evil, that I may not cause pain!" So God granted him what he requested. (1 Chronicles 4:9-10)

To tell you the truth, at first Jabez seemed like a pretty regular guy (kind of like me). But at the same time I could tell that God had done something really big with his life. I slowly read again that prayer Jabez had prayed. It was a very short prayer—only four lines. But for some reason it stuck with me like glue.

Only four lines. But for some reason it stuck with me like glue.

The next morning I prayed the little prayer myself—word for word, just as Jabez had done so many years ago. And then I prayed it the next morning, too.

And the next.

And the next.

And the next.

Thirty years later, I still pray that little prayer. And it's

amazing how this prayer has made what could've been just an ordinary life into something much, much more! I know it can do the same for you, because I know God is just waiting to give you more—much, much more—than you have ever thought to ask Him for.

Just ask Jabez.

WHERE'S JABEZ?

Maybe you remember the "Where's Waldo?" books. Perhaps you used to hunt for that funny-looking guy wearing the red-and-white-striped

A LITTLE GUY WITH GIANT-SIZED FAITH

REMEMBER the story of the shepherd boy? David was the least of his family; all seven brothers were older, stronger, and taller. And while they went off doing exciting things like fighting Israel's great battles, David's job was to run errands and care for his father's sheep. But David took his work seriously. He even risked his own life to fight off lions and bears! But where did he find this kind of confidence?

David, like our friend Jabez, took God seriously. He believed he could do anything with God's help. And more than that, he believed God *wanted* to help him. When the day came for someone to stand up to the brutal Philistine giant who had defied Israel's army, David, the little shepherd boy, bravely volunteered for the task. But of course, everyone thought he was crazy. How could a scrawny kid possibly defeat the fierce Goliath?

Yet David, with his giant-sized faith, stood confidently before the mighty warrior. Armed with only a sling and five smooth stones, David cried out, "I come to you in the name of the Lord God! He will give me the victory!"

You probably know the rest of the story. God gave David the victory, and the young boy killed the mighty giant with one small stone. Pretty amazing, isn't it? Little guy makes it big! In the time it took to throw a single stone, David went from lowly shepherd boy to national hero and stepped from an ordinary humdrum existence into a life full of excitement and adventure!

shirt who was always lost in the middle of a huge crowd. On every single page, Waldo was hidden somewhere in the midst of hundreds—maybe thousands—of other people, animals, and stuff. Readers would search every inch of each illustration until they finally spotted him.

Well, that's kind of like Jabez. He's tucked back in the Bible in the middle of the Old Testament, in the middle of 1 Chronicles, a book that hardly anyone ever reads because it's mostly just a bunch of boring lists. I'll bet you've never even opened this book of the Bible before.

So what exactly is Jabez's story?

If a book like 1 Chronicles were written today, it might sound like this: Donna and John Davis had two kids named Joshua and Amanda; then Amanda had three kids named Nicholas, Megan, and Hannah; and Amanda's brother, Joshua, had three kids named Alexandra, Tyler, and

Zach . . . yada, yada, yada . . . blah, blah, blah. Not exactly a page-turner, is it? But it's even worse in 1 Chronicles because the names sound like diseases or something you'd say after somebody sneezed—names like Ahumai, Ishma, Idbash, Hazelelponi. . . . You get the picture?

The point is: There, in the midst of these long, boring lists of names, you find poor Jabez—just stuck in the middle, kind of like Waldo. Except that it's not simply his name listed there with all the others. No, here's where it gets a little more interesting. Jabez gets his whole story told—right in the middle of all these boring lists. Kind of mysterious, isn't it? Now you might be wondering, So what exactly is Jabez's story?

Well, I'm glad you asked. As you may remember, his story starts out by announcing, "Jabez was more honorable than his brothers." The word *honorable* can mean several things—all good, of course. It might mean that Jabez lived a good and upright life, or that he was an important or wealthy man, or that people who knew him gave

Everyone can be a nuisance sometimes, but how would you like to be called Pain every day, 24/7?

him honor. That all sounds pretty good, doesn't it?

But life probably didn't start out well for Jabez. The next line tells us how his mother named him Jabez because he was born in pain. You see, the name Jabez *means* "pain." And that suggests something was hurtful when Jabez was born. Now, everyone can be a nuisance sometimes, but how would you like to be called Pain every day, twenty-four/seven?

Jabez didn't let this tough beginning stop him, though. We know that because in the next line, we hear him praying to God. He says, "Oh, that You would bless me indeed, and enlarge my territory, that Your hand would be with me, and that You would keep me from evil, that I may not cause pain!"

When you think about it, that's quite a bold prayer, isn't it? What made Jabez think God would do all those great things for an everyday guy like him? A guy whose name meant pain? But you know what? God did it! God answered Jabez's prayer. Pause and consider that fact for a moment. We've just met this guy named Jabez. He's an ordinary guy, and yet there's something special about him. What is it?

Maybe, like Jabez, you don't like your name, and some mean kid calls you Barf-Face for short.

Because of his name, we know Jabez's life started out

with some problems. And who doesn't have any problems? Sometimes our problems may seem so overwhelming they keep us from doing something really great with our lives. Maybe, like

Jabez, you don't like your name. Maybe it's an old-fashioned name like Bartholomew, and some mean kid calls you Barf-Face for short.

Or perhaps you don't like the way you look— you wish you were taller or shorter, or you don't like your freckles, or you wish you didn't have braces or glasses. Or maybe your family has problems; maybe your parents just got divorced, and you suddenly feel torn in two. Or perhaps you get teased at school for something you can't do a thing about.

Well, guess what. Things haven't changed all that much since the time of Jabez. We all have problems! We all have situations in our lives that seem totally unfair. But if we follow Jabez's example, we won't let our problems become a giant brick wall that blocks our way.

You see, Jabez faced his problems head-on. He came before God and did a very brave thing. He asked God to do something completely radical with his little, ho-hum life. And that's when Jabez's life changed. That little prayer made a gigantic difference in his life. Let's take a closer look at the prayer:

"Oh, that You would bless me indeed,
and enlarge my territory,
that Your hand would be with me,
and that You would keep me from evil. . . ."

So, what's up with these four simple requests? Sure, they sound good and nice. But what makes them so special? What's the big deal? Can you see it yet? Probably not. So read on, and I'll show you how simply praying this little prayer can turn your life into something really big.

CHAPTER TWO
So Why Not Ask?

 et's say you're at this really great youth camp where there's swimming and boating, dirt bikes and crafts, lots of great kids, and all kinds of fun stuff to do. But there's also this really cool counselor named Mario. You like listening to him because he's way funny, but he also seems to really know God—up close and personal. And you wonder how he got that way.

"Oh, that You would bless me indeed!"

So you're heading over to the mess hall one morning (the food's fantastic, and you don't want to be late—okay, we're imagining here) and you notice that Mario's cabin door is ajar. You spy him kneeling beside his bunk. He's praying. Now, even though you're starved, and you know it's rude to eavesdrop, you just can't resist. You pause outside Mario's door because you want to know what an amazing guy like Mario says when he prays. Does he ask God to bring world peace? Does he pray for the hungry and needy? Is he begging for a giant revival for the camp?

Isn't it rude to ask God for too many blessings for yourself?

You lean closer to listen, and this is what you hear him say: "Oh, God, I beg You, first of all this morning, please bless . . . *me!*"

Shocked that someone like Mario would pray such a self-ish prayer, you hurry along toward the mess hall. But just as you reach the door and smell the hotcakes you start to understand. Maybe important guys like Mario know something the rest of us don't. You

continue to think about Mario's prayer as you put
away a short stack of hotcakes, a glass of o.j., and
several pieces of bacon. Could the secret of Mario's
success be that he's not afraid to sound selfish—
that he's willing to ask God for whatever he wants?

As you walk back to your cabin, you wonder
what would happen if you did the same thing. Is
it possible that God wants you to pray more self-
ishly? But aren't you supposed to pray for those
in need? Isn't it rude to ask God for too many
blessings for yourself—kind of like handing your
parents a three-page Christmas list on the first
of December?

I want you to understand how praying this
way isn't selfish or greedy at all. I want you to
see how God is just waiting for you to come to
Him with this kind of request. It shows Him that
you really trust Him, that you believe He knows
what's best for you. It's just the kind of prayer
He loves to answer!

But first, let's take another look at our friend
Jabez.

A BIG REQUEST

LONG, LONG AGO, a woman named Hannah had a secret wish. All her life she had wanted a baby of her very own. Yet she continued to grow older without ever having a child. Each year, she and her husband traveled to a place called Shiloh to worship God. And each year she always hoped God would bless her with a baby. But year after year, nothing happened.

Finally, Hannah became old and gray—too old to think about having a baby. But she still hadn't given up her dream of a child. That year when Hannah arrived at Shiloh, she knelt down before God and prayed so hard that her lips moved and her body shook, but no words came out. The priest saw old Hannah trembling and shaking and wondered if she was drunk. "No," she assured him, "I'm just pouring my heart out to God."

And the old woman continued to pray like she'd never prayed before. "Dear God, if You'll just give me a son," she prayed silently, "I will give him back to serve You. I promise."

"May you find favor in God's eyes," said the priest as he passed by her.

When they could travel, old Hannah and her husband returned to Shiloh—this time to give thanks to God. For, indeed, He had blessed them. He had given Hannah a baby boy! They named the child Samuel, and Hannah kept her promise to God. Samuel grew up to be an important prophet for Israel. God used him to choose Israel's first kings and to share godly wisdom with the leaders. But what if Hannah had been afraid to ask God to do the impossible?

PAIN, NOT GAIN

It seems that Jabez lived in southern Israel. And he eventually grew up to become an important man—the head of his family. Only God knows the reason for his name. But it couldn't have been easy growing up with a label like that. After all, in those days, people took names seriously. And his name was a real pain! It's possible that bullies picked on him, and girls may have avoided him.

But the worst part for Jabez had to have been the way his name set him up for a sad, bleak future. Back then, your name could either make or break you. Like the two boys in the Bible named Mahlon and Chilion; their names meant "puny" and "pining," and they both died young. On a more positive note, there was Solomon, whose name meant "peace." Sure enough, he ruled Israel without ever going to war.

So Jabez had to realize his name was something of a handicap. He probably worried about what he had to look forward to. And yet Jabez rose above his gloomy prospects. Well aware of all the miracles God had done for his ancestors, Jabez believed God could do *anything*, no matter how big. He knew God could turn anything around—including his own insignificant, little life.

> Back then, your name could either make or break you.

So, Jabez may have figured, *Why not ask?*

That's exactly what he did. He asked God for something miraculous and totally impossible—something he could barely even imagine.

BLESSING ISN'T ABOUT SNEEZING

What comes to mind when you hear the word *bless* or *blessing?* Do you think of what your grandma says every time you sneeze? You go, "Aaah-*choo!*" and she says, "Bless you, dear." Or do you remember your pastor saying: "Let's ask God to bless those missionaries . . ."? Or perhaps your family asks a "blessing" before you eat a meal.

Does the idea of blessing seem sort of confusing to you? You're not alone. Most people don't realize the incredible power that's hidden in a real blessing—a blessing that only comes from God.

When we ask God to bless us, we invite Him to do something really huge and incredible—something we could never do for ourselves. We're asking Him to give to us from His unlimited

goodness and miraculous power. And that is no small thing!

Now, you may be thinking, *Hey, this is sounding pretty good. Does this mean I can ask God for whatever I want and—wham!—He'll just bless me with it?* Maybe you're already entertaining thoughts of a new motorized scooter or that latest video game or a faster computer or even a real, live horse! After all, God's resources are unlimited, right?

Does this mean I can ask God for whatever I want and—wham!—He'll just bless me with it?

But let's go back to Jabez. Remember the way he asked God to bless him? He didn't tell God *how* to bless him (other than a lot!). Instead Jabez left the possibilities wide open. He left it up to God to decide. You see, Jabez trusted God completely. And he wanted nothing less than God's best for him.

Think about it. What if Jabez had specifically asked God to bless him with, say, a really nice house? And suppose God did. But what if God had really wanted to bless him with an enormous palace? Jabez would've cut himself short by telling God exactly *how* to bless him.

When we ask for God's blessing—and trust Him to do it *His* way—we won't be disappointed. This is how it works: We allow God to lead us, and then we pray for what God desires. And suddenly all sorts of miraculous things begin to happen. No, I don't mean God showers down all sorts of material things. Because, think about it: What are the best parts of your life anyway? Usually not stuff, not material things.

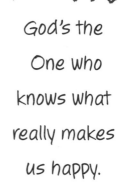

God's the One who knows what really makes us happy.

You see, God's the One who knows what really makes us happy, and He knows exactly how to do it. But this can only happen when we trust Him, when we truly believe that He wants what's best for us—when we say, "Okay, God, I want what You want!" Then, before we know it, God's doing amazing things. That's just the way God works!

GOD WANTS TO BLESS US

We all have different ideas of how we think God wants to bless us. Some think that once you become a Christian, God's blessings just trickle down on you like gentle spring showers without any effort or asking on your part.

Others think that receiving God's blessings is like being in a prize-drawing giveaway. They think if they get too many blessings, they aren't allowed to "win" again for a while—or even that God would send trouble their way to balance out all the great things He has given them.

And some might think they actually earn God's blessings by doing something good. They do a good deed, and—*puh-ching!* (like a cash register)—God drops a little blessing from the sky. Payoff time.

But those ideas are nonsense. God is God. And He is so incredibly good and generous and kind that despite who we are or what we do, He wants to bless us anyway, simply because of who He is! His resources, power, and willingness to give to us are more unlimited than the grains of sand on the earth or the stars in the sky! His only limitation is us—when we don't ask.

It's time to change our way of thinking about God. It's time to understand that He's ready and waiting for us all. He wants to give good gifts to His children. So what's stopping us? Can we be as brave as Jabez? Can we stand before God and ask Him to bless us?

Why not make a lifelong commitment today? Why not decide that, from now on, you will ask God every single day to bless you—and while He's at it—to *bless you a lot!*

It doesn't matter who you are, what your name is, or where you come from. All it takes is a simple prayer of faith. If you really believe God knows what's the very best for you, and if you're willing to ask Him for it, then some great changes are right around the corner. Like our friend Jabez, you can have a future that's brighter than you could ever imagine. Just think: Your life can begin to change one minute from now!

CHAPTER THREE
Living Big for God

he next part of the Jabez prayer is asking God to make our lives bigger so that we might do more for Him.

"And enlarge my territory."

When he prayed his prayer, Jabez wasn't thinking only in terms of acreage. No! Jabez wanted to have more influence and bigger responsibilities. He wanted a bigger opportunity to *make a mark for God.*

Having more land was a part of being an influence. Back in the days of Jabez, a nation or a man was measured by the amount of land owned and occupied. The bigger the better! Perhaps Jabez looked over his spread of land and thought, *I was born for more than this! My God is bigger than this!*

If you
really know
who God is,
you know the
options are
unlimited.

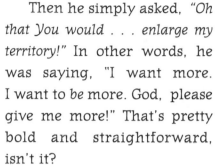

Then he simply asked, *"Oh that You would . . . enlarge my territory!"* In other words, he was saying, "I want more. I want to be more. God, please give me more!" That's pretty bold and straightforward, isn't it?

Now, what if Jabez were your age in this time? What do you think he would ask God for? Let's suppose he'd love surfing the Web, and he'd really want to set up his own Web site. Maybe he'd ask God to help him get what he needed to develop his home page. Then he'd use his site to tell others how great God is.

Or what if Jabez lived in the city and wished that he and his friends could find a cool place where they could get together and play sports and do fun stuff? Maybe he'd ask God to give him a great facility to use as a gathering place for him and his friends—a place where they could learn more about God and reach out to even more kids.

Who knows what Jabez might've asked for? He might have simply asked to be blessed. He knew the options were unlimited, and he knew that God was ready to give. God is still ready to give without limits. You just need to be bold enough to ask.

Or maybe you're thinking this all sounds good—really good. But you're thinking maybe it sounds too good to be true. So maybe you're a little bit afraid to ask. Maybe you're afraid if you ask, God might not answer. Then you would feel let down—or perhaps even embarrassed.

THE SAD SURPRISE

One fine spring day, Andy McIntyre discovered it was his day to go to heaven. (Let's face it, this happens to all of us sooner or later.) Andy was ready to meet his Maker. After all, he'd known Jesus since second grade. But when Andy got his first glimpse of heaven, he was totally amazed by the beauty and wonder of the place.

"Hello," said Saint Peter as he met Andy at the pearly gates. "Are you ready for the tour?"

"Oh yeah!" said Andy with wide eyes.

Well, Peter showed Andy the incredible streets of pure gold. He showed him the beautiful River of Life, the buildings made of millions of precious gemstones, and all sorts of fantastic places and celestial wonders. But one particular building caught Andy's eye.

"What's that place?" asked Andy as he looked up at the gigantic building. It resembled an enormous warehouse with no windows and only one door.

"Oh, it's just a storage building," said Saint Peter. "I'm sure you're not interested in that."

"A storage building?" Andy looked up toward the rooftop. "Why, it must be ten stories tall— what's in there?"

"Oh, just some things that nobody ever used," explained Saint Peter, turning away. "No big deal."

But Andy's curiosity was growing. "Please, may I see what's inside?" he begged.

Saint Peter nodded sadly then opened the door. "Go ahead and take a look around."

"He was just waiting for them to ask."

Andy stepped inside and saw rows and rows of shelves—so tall they reached to the ceiling. And on each shelf were stacks of white gift boxes, each one tied with a bright red ribbon.

Andy read the name tags on the boxes near him—Joseph Abby, Michaela Abdullah, Travis Abernathy. He turned to Saint Peter. "Do all these boxes have names on them?"

Saint Peter sighed and said, "Yes."

"Is there one here for me?" asked Andy, his eyes wide with excitement.

"Yes. It would be in the M section."

Andy rushed through the building, searching

for the M section. Finally, he found the white box with his name on it—Andrew James McIntyre.

"May I open it?" he asked Saint Peter happily.

He nodded. "You might as well."

Andy opened the box, and his smile faded. "But—what's this?" he stammered. "I—I never knew." Then he let out a deep, sad sigh, like the sighs Saint Peter had heard from so many others.

"You see, all these boxes are the gifts that God wants to give His children," Saint Peter explained. "He's just waiting for them to ask."

Andy stared at his unclaimed blessings and was flooded with disappointment. "But I never did. I never asked."

Saint Peter looked at Andy and sadly shook his head. "Most people don't."

Andy studied the wonderful contents of the box with dismay. "Oh, man . . . I wish I had asked."

Now, of course, that's just a fictional story, but it reminds us of all the blessings God might have in store for us—if we would just ask. It's not like we can guess what might be in a box like that. After all, God's the giver. What the gift contains is up to Him. But we can be sure that whatever He has for us will be good—very, very good. We just need to ask.

THINK BIGGER

One time I spoke to about 2,000 college students for a whole week. I challenged them to join me in praying the prayer of Jabez. Then I took it up a notch.

"Why don't you all look at the globe and pick an island," I suggested. "Then put together a team of students, charter an airliner, and take over the island for God."

Some of them roared with laughter. Some of them thought I was nuts. But they all listened as I continued to speak. "Why don't you ask God for the island of Trinidad?" I said. I had just been there and had seen that it was a place of wonderful opportunity. "And while you're at it," I added, "ask God to give you a DC-10, too."

Well, not one person offered to take me up on this challenge. But the students did start talking about things they might do. And most of them really wanted to do something bigger and better with their lives. They just didn't know where to begin. Usually, they got hung up on all the things they didn't have—like money or skill or courage or opportunity.

I kept asking those college kids a question, and it's the same question I'm going to ask you right now.

Are you ready?

If God loves you so much, why has He left you down here?

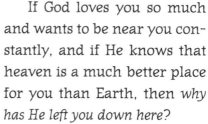

If God loves you so much and wants to be near you constantly, and if He knows that heaven is a much better place for you than Earth, then *why has He left you down here?*

Okay, here's the answer I gave them. This is the same answer I offer you: I believe you are on Earth because God wants you to be moving out your boundary lines. He wants you to take in new territory for Him. That means telling people about Jesus and how to grow to be more like Him. Ask God to bring people into your life so you can tell them about Him, and you may be surprised who responds first! Maybe it's a member of the soccer team. Or maybe it's the entire team. Maybe it's your next-door neighbor—or your whole town. What an honor to realize God has put you on Earth because He wants you to do big things for Him. That's why you're here!

Well, those college students started praying the Jabez prayer, and let me tell you, things started changing. By the next fall, they had launched a mission they called "Operation Jabez." They got 126 students together, and they chartered a jet, and—you guessed it—they went to Trinidad! All 126 of them for the whole summer!

Now, you might not be ready to charter a plane, fly off to an island, and tell everyone about Jesus. But God has something for you to do—something bigger and better than anything you've ever considered. But you need to ask Him, and then you need to step out in faith.

God has something for you to do— something bigger and better than anything you've ever considered before.

TWO GUYS WITH BIG FAITH

DO YOU REMEMBER the story about how God used Moses to lead the children of Israel out of captivity in Egypt? He performed all sorts of incredible miracles—sent plagues of frogs and pests, and even divided the great Red Sea so they could cross on dry ground.

Where was God leading them? To the Promised Land—a fantastic place filled with marvelous gifts for them.

However, when they finally reached the borders of the Promised Land, the children of Israel got nervous. They'd heard some scary stories about this place—tales of giants and walled fortresses and worse. And suddenly they weren't so eager to move into the Promised Land.

"It looks really good," they said, "but it's too hard."

Two men stood up to the crowd that day. They both desperately wanted to go into the Promised Land. They both believed that, despite the challenges, God would take care of them there. They knew God was big enough to handle anything—including giants!

"God will protect us!" cried Caleb. "He has promised to give us this land. We just need to go in there and get what is ours."

Still the people were worried and afraid.

"Listen to Caleb," cried Joshua. "He's right! That land is full of lots of good food and things we need. God has given it to us. We just need to have faith and go in and claim it."

Still the people refused to go. As a result, they never got to live in the Promised Land. Instead they wandered around the wilderness for decades. Out of all those people, only Joshua and Caleb were allowed into the Promised Land—but even they had to wait forty years first. God must've been disappointed.

GOD'S MATH ADDS UP

There is one thing all Christians have in common, no matter who we are, what we look like, or where we live or go to school. Whether we're rich or poor or somewhere in between, God wants each of us to represent Him. The way He reveals His love, His mercy, and His kindness to others is through us. We're like His hands.

Unfortunately, our hands, which could do God's work on Earth, feel tied or sat upon or hidden behind our backs. Do you know why that is? Usually it's because we don't think we have *enough* to do what needs to be done. But that's only because we're not adding things right. You see, this is how we add things up:

Who I am + what I know + my personality +
my looks + who people think I am =
how much territory I deserve.

But that's not how God adds things up. He uses ordinary people to do extraordinary things, so His math works different from ours. God knows what He's able to do when someone is willing. This is how we add things up using God's math:

My willingness + my lack of abilities +
God's will + God's power =
how much territory God wants to give me.

Do you see the difference there? God's just waiting for us to trust Him. Then He can lead us into new territory. That's what happened to a sixteen-year-old named Taylor. He started praying the prayer of Jabez after his youth minister shared it with his church group. Every day Taylor asked God to enlarge his territory, but a few days went by before he noticed a change—and then it seemed like a change for the worse! One terrible Saturday, someone let the air out of Taylor's tire while he was at work, and

We don't think we have enough because we're not adding things right.

that evening his girlfriend broke up with him. He felt crushed. Then something interesting happened. Twenty minutes after his girlfriend said good-bye, he had an unexpected opportunity to "enlarge his territory." His brother's friend casually asked Taylor if he would talk to him about becoming a Christian. The friend accepted Christ that very night!

Then, a couple of days later, Taylor started talking with a guy he met—a former gang member who had been living a wild life—and that night he accepted Christ, too! The next day someone who had been Taylor's good friend in middle school told him, "I want what you have. I want to become a Christian."

Taylor went from feeling like dirt to soaring over the top of the mountain. Three territory additions in five days! "That week was amazing," Taylor recalled. "Even when everything seemed to be going wrong, God still found ways to bring me up." Today Taylor says, "When you pray the prayer of Jabez, get ready for something to happen. I'm only sixteen, and God uses me in ways I thought I could never be used!"

Taylor's right. God can use us to do things we never thought possible. But we have to be willing. Remember Joshua and Caleb? They understood the way God adds things up. They knew God would give them the Promised Land. They knew it was theirs for the taking. They were eager and willing to go. But the rest of the people added things in a human way. As a result they never got to set foot in the Promised Land.

So why not ask God to expand your territory? Just think of the great things He has in store for you. He will lead and guide you. You don't have to worry. All you need is willingness. Excitement lies ahead!

CHAPTER FOUR
God's Helping Hand

Now you've gone and done it. Gotten in over your head—plunged into the deep end. You've prayed the prayer of Jabez, taken God at His word—and *boom!*—things have started to happen. And they're happening fast!

Maybe you've told a couple of friends at school about God, and suddenly they have a bunch of questions—tough questions! Or maybe you started a small after-school Bible study, and rapidly the group tripled in size. *Now* what are you going to do? Or perhaps your church youth group began a new project, and things started moving so fast that it got a little scary.

"That Your hand would be with me."

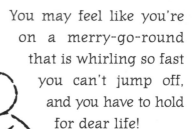

You may feel like you're on a merry-go-round that is whirling so fast you can't jump off, and you have to hold for dear life!

It's possible to be blessed by God and to become so amazed by His power that you get caught in a sort of whirlwind. Before you know it, you feel overwhelmed. Or unexpected problems crop up, and you wonder if you may have heard God wrong. Or maybe someone criticizes your efforts, and you feel let down. Or perhaps someone is jealous of your success and, as a result, hurts your feelings.

You see, when God blesses us and expands our territory, there's no promise that everything's going to be smooth and simple. Exciting? Definitely! Easy? No way! But think about it . . . how many great things in life come easily? Is it easy to win a gold medal at the Olympics? Was it simple to land a man on the moon? No! In the same way, living the life God wants us to live might be the most difficult thing you have ever tried to do.

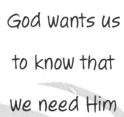

God wants us to know that we need Him desperately!

So, maybe you're thinking, *Why bother? If it's that hard, how can anyone do it?* And the answer is: No one can do it.

Not without God's help. You see, God wants us to know that we need Him desperately!

After all, we're working to carry out God's plans. And there's no way we can do this work on our own. God wants us to depend on Him for everything. We need His power, His wisdom, His guidance . . . His *everything!* We simply cannot do His work on our own without failing miserably or making a complete mess of things. And this is where we come to the next line of our Jabez prayer:

"That your hand would be with me."

Somehow Jabez knew he'd need God's hand to help him through the hard times, to pick him up when he fell, and to give him the strength and courage to continue.

A HELPING HAND

Imagine that you're climbing a mountain for the first time, and you've stopped on a dangerous ledge. You look down to the staggering depths

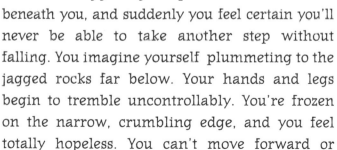

You're frozen on the narrow, crumbling edge, and you feel totally hopeless.

beneath you, and suddenly you feel certain you'll never be able to take another step without falling. You imagine yourself plummeting to the jagged rocks far below. Your hands and legs begin to tremble uncontrollably. You're frozen on the narrow, crumbling edge, and you feel totally hopeless. You can't move forward or

"It's okay.

I've got you.

Just move

forward."

backward, and you just don't know what to do.

Then your guide (an older, much more experienced mountaineer) reaches out and grips your hand. He looks you in the eyes and says, "It's okay. I've got you. Just move forward slowly . . . one foot at a time." Clinging to his hand, you inch across the ledge until you finally reach solid ground. Without his help, you never would have made it. Just the grasp of his hand empowered you to continue.

It's like that with God's helping hand, too—only more so. The Bible describes God's hand in differing ways. In the Old Testament, "the hand of God" symbolizes His power and presence in the lives of His people (see Joshua 4:24 and Isaiah 59:1). In the New Testament, "the hand of the Lord" refers to God's Holy Spirit (see Acts 11:21). The purpose of the Holy Spirit is to empower ordinary believers to do extraordinary things. In other words, God's hand on our lives helps us to go and do and be more than we ever dreamed possible.

What a relief to know it's not *our* power and strength that accomplish great things! It's God's hand. We can do nothing on our own. That's why we want to always pray that He keeps His hand on us. To be without God's hand is like freezing with fear on that narrow rock ledge with nowhere to turn.

Now, you still may feel a little nervous when your first Jabez opportunity pops up. If you're like most of us, you'll worry that you don't know what to say or that you'll say too much and embarrass yourself. Yes, it's scary out on that ledge! But before you begin, take a second, draw in a breath, and pray silently, *That Your hand would be with me!* Then . . . just begin, confident that God is in control. Keep it simple. Give the other person a chance to ask a question. And enjoy the moment as you feel God working through you to touch someone's life!

THE LITTLE BIG MAN

PERHAPS you've heard of Gideon. He was one of Israel's great leaders. But when God picked him for the job, Gideon responded by saying, "Oh, God, You know I'm the least in my family—and my family is the lowest family in all Israel."

And you know what God said to Gideon?

"I will be with you. And you will defeat the Midianites *as one man."*

Whew! *As one man.* That must've been some pretty heady stuff for a nobody like Gideon.

Well, after that encounter, a number of things happened to convince Gideon that God was, indeed,

with him. And before long, Gideon's confidence grew. Not only that, but the confidence of the people of Israel grew as well. They had thought of Gideon as floor dust. But with God's hand on him, Gideon quickly turned into a "somebody." So when the time came to prepare for the biggest battle of Gideon's career, he had no problem getting volunteers. In fact, thousands of brave warriors eagerly joined him for the huge battle.

But God made Gideon cut back the size of his troops until only 300 men remained. Then God instructed Gideon to take along trumpets and empty pitchers to use against the enormous armies of warriors "as numerous as locusts, and their camels without number." Gideon followed God's instructions, and at the right moment, the trumpets blasted and the pitchers were broken. Hearing the commotion, the enemy armies were so rattled that they fled the battlefield and defeated themselves!

God proved His hand was upon Gideon by stacking the odds against his army. It's easy to imagine how thankful Gideon must have felt after miraculously winning this victory. He could *only* have won by the hand of God!

TWELVE TEENS AND A MIRACLE

Many years ago, I was a youth pastor in New Jersey. One summer, twelve kids and I decided to

People from our church said it was impossible. And they were right. It was.

do something big for God. We set our sights on Long Island, New York. Our objective: to make God known to all the kids in that area.

We put together a three-part plan. During the day, we'd meet with kids in backyard gatherings and on the beach. In the evenings, we'd hold meetings in local churches. It sounded like a good plan, but before summer came, we began to feel overwhelmed. We invited an expert in youth ministries to come talk to us.

He said if we got thirteen or fourteen kids together in a backyard, we should consider that a total success.

After he left I said, "You know, our work would be a success if we led one person to the Lord, but . . . I think we should expect *one hundred* kids." Well, you should've seen their faces! *One hundred kids?* That sounded like a miracle just waiting to happen. Suddenly we knew it was time to pray. We asked God to bless us, and we asked Him to give us one hundred kids. We asked Him to do something miraculous—for His own glory.

But the impossible began to happen right before our very eyes.

People from our church said it was impossible. And they were right. It was. But once our summer ministry began, the impossible began to happen right before our very eyes. We had hundreds of kids showing up for our backyard meetings. Our crowds on the beach were even larger.

By the time we finished our six weeks on Long Island, we could count 1,200 new believers! Do the math: That's one hundred believers per teen! It was a miracle!

He's got all the power in the universe; He just needs our willingness to partner with Him.

When those twelve teens went home that summer, they knew that *God could do anything!* And remember the doubters at our home church? Well, those same twelve teens began praying for the doubtful, and, as a result, a huge revival swept through our church as well. All because twelve ordinary kids asked God to bless them and extend their outreach—not forgetting to ask that His hand of power be on them as well!

God is looking for more people like that—ordinary people who believe Him. People who are loyal and take Him at His word. He's got all the power in the universe; He just needs our willingness to partner with Him.

Sometimes we'll partner with God in a huge project that involves saving hundreds of kids, and sometimes we'll partner with Him to share the gospel with just one person. Sometimes we'll reach out to the kid who is hurting in our class, and sometimes we'll just share a smile to encourage all who are struggling. All results are miracles—miracles that only God can bring to pass. How thrilling that He wants us to partner with Him!

CHAPTER FIVE

The Safety Zone

An interesting magazine ad shows a picture of a Roman gladiator. Normally, we think of gladiators as fierce warriors, but this guy's in big trouble. Somehow, he's dropped his sword, and a ferocious (and probably hungry) lion is in mid-lunge, jaws opened wide. The crowd in the coliseum is on its feet, watching in horror as the frightened gladiator tries to get away. The caption for the ad reads, "Sometimes you can afford to come in second. Sometimes you can't."

After praying for God's blessing and for more territory and for God to keep His hand on him, you might just assume that Jabez would be feeling brave enough to jump

"That You would keep me from evil."

into anything—even a coliseum with a hungry lion. Or you might expect that Jabez would use the final line of his prayer to ask God to care for him and protect him as he passed through evil—since everyone knows there's plenty of evil in this world.

But Jabez took the last line of his prayer up another decibel by asking that God would "keep him from evil." That's another pretty bold request.

It seems Jabez understood something that the gladiator in the ad didn't know: The best way to defeat the lion is to stay out of the ring altogether. Jabez used the last line of his prayer to ask God to just keep him out of the fight. Period.

Pretty smart, wasn't it? How can you get beat

up if you don't get caught in the middle of the skirmish? But that's exactly what Satan wants us to do. He wants us to be pulled into a nasty battle where we'll lose.

KEEPING A SAFE DISTANCE

It's no secret that as soon as we begin living our lives for God, Satan gets mad. And when he gets mad, things can get really ugly. It's just a fact of the spiritual life. But we don't have to be pulled into the ugliness. We don't have to get caught in the fray. There's a way to keep a safe distance.

Do you remember how Jesus taught His disciples to pray? We call it the Lord's Prayer, and one important line of this prayer is very similar to the line in Jabez's prayer.

Jesus taught His disciples to ask, "And do not lead us into temptation, but deliver us from the evil one" (Matthew 6:13). Do you notice that Jesus didn't ask us to become mighty spiritual warriors and defeat Satan with our powerful words or brave deeds? No, He knew us better than that. He just asked that we wouldn't get pulled toward what tempts us. Here's a Bible verse that says it in plain English: "Resist the devil and he will flee from you" (James 4:7). The word *resist* means "to stand against" or "to abstain from"—especially

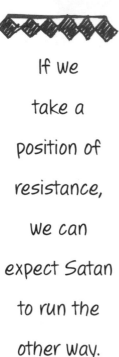

If we take a position of resistance, we can expect Satan to run the other way.

when it comes to temptation. So if we take a position of resistance, we can expect Satan to run the other way. Sounds pretty good, doesn't it? It's kind of like staying in God's safety zone.

Have you ever witnessed the last seconds of a very close football game? Say it's the state championship, and your team is ahead by one measly point. There are eleven seconds left, and your team has the ball—just seventeen yards from your end zone. That other team wants to win this game badly; you can see it in the players' eyes. If they can intercept that football, they're gonna cross those seventeen yards and be in that end zone before your team knows what's happened. *What's your team gonna do?*

Play it safe, of course. They'll hold tight to the ball, protect their ball-handler with the rest of the offense, and not take any risks as they watch the clock run out. Then they'll win! All because they did their best and played it safe in the crucial moments.

It's kind of like that with us. God knows we need to stay in His safety zone so that we don't get beat up and lose the game. Whether or not we like to admit it, we're not strong enough to defeat the enemy—at least not on our own.

THREE RESISTERS

DO YOU REMEMBER the story of those three guys who got the hot seat—Shadrach, Meshach, and Abednego? They were Israelites held captive in Babylon (an empire that didn't believe in God). And when the king of Babylon built a huge golden statue (an idol), he expected everyone in his kingdom to worship it—including the Israelites.

Now, this king had quite a worship program going. He had appointed special musicians to play a certain kind of music, and whenever this music played, everyone was supposed to fall

down and worship his gigantic gold idol.

Anyone who refused would be tossed into a custom-made furnace where the guards could crank up the temperature high enough to melt heavy metal. Consider the choices here—to just bow down whenever the king's silly music played, or to be thrown into a fiery furnace that would melt the flesh from your bones. It must've been tempting for everyone to consider kneeling and pretending to worship the idol.

But Shadrach, Meshach, and Abednego didn't give in to that temptation. They told the king they served the living God, and they refused to worship the king's idol. That's when things started getting hot. The furious king ordered the furnace to be heated seven times hotter than normal, and the three men were thrown inside.

But Shadrach, Meshach, and Abednego weren't even scorched. Not only that, but a fourth man was seen walking amid the flames with them. (Some say it was Jesus keeping them company.) Needless to say, the king was totally shocked when they finally walked out and didn't even smell like smoke! After that, the king praised and honored the living God, and things started to change around Babylon.

We're not

strong

enough

to defeat

the enemy—

at least not

on our own.

But there are "safe" choices we make every day that keep us out of harm's way.

When temptation comes (and it will) we can ask for God's help, and He'll make us strong enough to stand firm and brave enough to turn and walk away.

It's not always easy to walk away from temptation, is it? The tricky thing about temptation is that it's so *tempting*. Temptation is like poison disguised as a hot-fudge sundae. It can look really good on the outside. In fact, it looks scrumptious, but its effects can make you really sick.

Whether your temptation comes in the form of friends trying to get you to do something wrong or in the form of a habit that God has asked you to break, some form of temptation is always just around the corner. That's why it's better to keep a safe distance.

FORCED INTO THE FIGHT

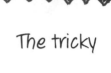

Now, even though we pray that God will keep evil from us, times will still come when we're forced into some form of spiritual battle. The important thing to remember is that this is not our *own personal battle*. Satan just wants us to think it is. Remember, he's a big fat liar.

The truth is *Jesus has already defeated Satan*. The way we stand up to Satan is to remember that Jesus won the battle

The tricky thing about temptation is that it's so tempting.

for us when He rose from the dead. It's only because of what Jesus did that we can stand up to Satan now.

A PATHETIC ENEMY

Some places in Scripture describe Satan as a hungry lion, prowling about the earth and looking for someone to destroy. It's a vivid image, and pretty scary too. After all, who wants to come face to face with a fierce lion that hasn't eaten in weeks?

But let's weigh this image against the defeating blow that Jesus dealt when He died and arose from the dead. Yes, Satan is still a lion, still on the prowl, and he's certainly eager to destroy someone. But what we need to remember is that he's now a lion who's been declawed. Unless we fall victim to his trickery and lies, we're pretty safe. Our best bet is to just turn and walk away. Remember: If we resist, Satan flees.

PROTECTING OUR TURF

After Jabez began to experience God's blessing and saw his territory increase, you can bet he wanted to make sure he kept it safe. He realized the enormity of what he'd been given. It's no

different with us. As we become more aware of what God's doing in our lives—aware of the ways He's using us to reach others—then we won't want to risk it either. And that's what this portion of the prayer is all about.

Do you believe God can keep you from evil?

Do you believe God can keep you from evil? Do you believe He wants to protect you, as well as protect what He's doing in your life? Then go ahead—pray that fourth line of Jabez's prayer and really mean it!

"That You would keep me from evil."

Now you're ready to see what God can do as He continues to increase the blessings in your life . . . as He continues to expand your borders . . . as He keeps His hand on you. Prepare to be amazed!

CHAPTER SIX
Welcome to God's Honor Roll

Have you ever had a teacher who seemed to favor one particular student? Maybe that student got called "teacher's pet." That kind of favoritism probably didn't seem fair, did it?

What about God? Do you think He has favorites? He did seem to favor Jabez over his brothers. But that doesn't really make sense because we know God loves everyone equally—and Jesus died for everyone, not just a favored few.

Yet Scripture says, "Jabez was more honorable" than the rest. So could it be that God really *does* have favorites? Do you remember all those other people listed before

Jabez was more honorable than his brothers.

and after Jabez—the ones with names that sounded like tropical diseases? Idbash, Hazelelponi, Anub, and the others? We don't see any honors or awards listed next to their names. So why didn't God favor them too?

Well, here's the clincher: *God does favor those who ask.*

When we want to do what He wants us to do, our lives become more exciting.

God doesn't hold back from those people who really want His will for their lives. You see, God loves it when we say, "Here I am, Lord. Do what You will with me." To God, that alone makes us "more honorable."

Now, being "more honorable" here on Earth might mean that we get more respect, have more talent, more money, more friends. But to God, it means something entirely different. To God, it means that how we live our lives brings more honor to Him.

So, you see, it's not selfish to be like Jabez and want to be "more honorable." It's a good thing, really. It's like wanting to be more loving, more giving, kinder . . . in other words, *more like our heavenly Father*. He loves it when His children try to imitate Him. It's a father's greatest joy! And when we *want* to do what *He* wants us to do, our lives become more exciting.

DIVINE APPOINTMENTS

If you're like most people your age, you probably don't carry a Day-Timer or a Palm Pilot and schedule lots of appointments throughout your day. Oh, sure, there are places you have to be—like soccer practice or the orthodontist or music lessons or youth group. But the idea of making and keeping an appointment with just one person for

FROM PRINCE TO PAUPER TO . . .

I'M SURE you remember Moses, the guy who went from baby-in-a-basket to prince of Egypt the day the Pharaoh's daughter pulled him out of the river. Well, as quickly as he rose to fame, he fell right out again when he killed a man that he'd caught abusing a Jewish slave. That's when Moses discovered that he too was Jewish, and he ran away from Egypt before things got worse.

Moses felt confused, miserable, and worthless. His whole identity had been shattered in the course of a single day. It felt like his life was over.

He became a lowly shepherd and for many years just minded his own business and took care of his father-in-law's sheep. But God had other plans for Moses. Despite the way Moses saw himself—as a nobody or loser who couldn't even talk very well—God knew He could use him.

So God called Moses to one of the biggest challenges of Bible history—a seemingly impossible task. God wanted Moses to deliver the nation of Israel from captivity in Egypt. Did Moses feel capable, trained, or equipped for this outrageous assignment?

Not at all! But God knew Moses' heart. And God also knew He'd picked the right man for the job.

Moses, empowered by God, did manage to do the impossible. After numerous confrontations and incredible miracles (performed by God), Moses forced Pharaoh to free all the Jewish slaves. Then, led by God, Moses delivered the whole Jewish nation out of captivity and away from Egypt.

Did God favor Moses? Of course He did! Because Moses had the right kind of heart, and he was willing to be used by God—even when he felt totally inadequate for the job.

one specific reason might seem kind of out there to you. But hang with me for a minute.

You see, I've come to believe that when I'm praying the prayer of Jabez, God gives me what I call *divine appointments*. For no explainable reason, my path will cross someone else's—and before I know it, miraculous things are happening. I believe these miraculous things can happen with you, too.

Here's how it works: You might be doing something ordinary like waiting for the school bus or standing in the lunch line or having halftime at a soccer game. Suddenly you see someone and feel compelled to say something to him or her. Maybe you don't even know the person's name, but for some reason you believe God wants you to say something. So you breathe in a quick little prayer and step forward—and your heart starts to pound.

Then one thing leads to another, and maybe you find out this person is really hurting inside—maybe the parents are having some marriage problems and the kid feels caught in the middle. But suddenly

My path will cross someone else's— and before I know it, miraculous things are happening.

So you
breathe in
a quick
little prayer
and step
forward—
and your
heart
starts
to pound.

you find you've made a new friend, and you're actually helping. And it feels good. Maybe you invite him or her to eat lunch with you, and the next thing you know, your new pal has agreed to come to youth group on Wednesday night.

And that, my friend, is what I call a divine appointment. It's something that only God can put together. He sets up a situation, and because you're in the right place at the right time—and tuned in to God—you're ready to participate in something really big!

Believe me, nothing is bigger than having God work through you to touch someone else. Just don't forget that He's working *through* you. That's the key. It is God's power and God's strength that make the whole thing special. And that takes the pressure off you. You don't have to be smart or attractive or popular for God to use you to reach someone else. You just have to be willing. Sound familiar? Yeah, there's definitely a pattern here. Throughout the Bible (and still today) God uses anyone who is willing. That's when miraculous things start to happen!

HOLD ON FOR THE RIDE!

So maybe you're thinking, *I like what's happening since I started praying this prayer of Jabez, but it's a little overwhelming.* Maybe things are happening fast, and your life is changing (in good ways), but it's frightening, too. Like on that whirling merry-go-round.

First, you need to remember that it's God who's in control. You just need to hold on to Him. (Actually, He's holding on to you.) You can know He'll keep things under control as long as you are trusting Him and doing things His way.

As you continue to pray the Jabez prayer on a daily basis, you'll continue to see God's touch on your life and the lives of those around you, and it will get bigger and better. Believe me, I've seen more miracles than this little book could contain. And it's an exciting way to live—being partners with God!

But there is one way we can foul things up, and that's by letting sin creep into our lives.

Remember line four of our prayer—it's the deal breaker. Never forget that sin stops God's power from flowing.

It's as if the electric lines in your house have been severed, and you're cut off from all those immense power generators owned by the power company. Vast amounts of power are still available at the power source, but until the lines to your house get fixed, you're just sitting in the dark.

If you've experienced the incredible Jabez blessing, you'll notice a huge difference when sin cuts off your power source. The good news is that God's just waiting for you to reconnect. He's ready to forgive you and help you get your life right back on track. Don't waste a minute getting reconnected to Him!

CHAPTER SEVEN
Making Jabez Mine

So God granted him what he requested.

I challenge you to make the prayer of Jabez a regular part of your day. To help you do this, I encourage you, for the next thirty days, to follow the plan I've made for you. I know thirty days might sound like a long time, but if you commit yourself to doing this, I think you'll be thrilled with the changes you see. Just as with your sport or your homework, when you practice repeatedly, before long, it feels natural. And eventually, it's easier.

When you see what God's doing because of your prayers, I'm sure you'll want the Jabez prayer to be a part of the rest of your life.

HERE'S THE PLAN:

1. Make a calendar or chart to mark off each day that you pray the Jabez prayer. Pray this prayer every day.

2. Write out the Jabez prayer and tape it somewhere where you'll see it every day (like on your mirror or your door or wherever).

3. Reread this little book once a week during the first thirty days. Ask God to show you anything important that you might have missed the first time.

4. Tell one other person about your commitment to pray the Jabez prayer. Ask him or her to check on your progress.

5. Keep a little notebook handy to list any changes in your life, like blessings or divine appointments or anything else that you feel may be a result of the prayer of Jabez.

6. Start praying the Jabez prayer for your family, friends, and church.

7. Get some of your friends to start praying the prayer of Jabez for the next thirty days, too!

Of course, what you *know* about this or any other prayer won't get you anything. And you can hang the Jabez prayer on every wall of your house and nothing will happen. It's not a lucky charm.

It's when you really *believe* that God wants to release His blessings and power—only then will you experience the life-changing effects of the Jabez prayer. That's when you really step up to God's best for you.

THE LIFE YOU'RE MEANT TO LEAD

Sure, you may be "just a kid." But that doesn't make you any less important in God's eyes. To God we're all the same, no matter our age or size or qualifications. He's just looking for hearts that want to serve Him. And God has awesome things in store for you—not for someday when you're all grown up, but for right now! *Today!*

God wants us to live the lives we're meant to lead—starting now. And the only way we can discover this life is to come before God and ask Him. That's what the prayer of Jabez is all about.

It brings us before our heavenly Father as we ask Him with great hope and expectation to make our ordinary lives into something incredible and fantastic, beyond our wildest imaginings. He's just waiting to give us the life we're meant to live. He's just waiting to release His miraculous power in our lives. For now and for all eternity, God wants to pour out His honor and delight on us! So, what are we waiting for?

And Jabez called on the God of Israel saying,
"Oh, that You would bless me indeed,
and enlarge my territory,
that Your hand would be with me,
and that You would keep me from evil,
that I may not cause pain!"
So God granted him what he requested.
(1 Chronicles 4:10)